AF374783

PHANATHEMA
&
THE PRINCESS

A collection of poems

A N T H O N Y   J .   L E C K N E R

BALBOA.PRESS

A DIVISION OF HAY HOUSE

Balboa Press books may be ordered through booksellers or by contacting:

Balboa Press
A Division of Hay House
1663 Liberty Drive
Bloomington, IN 47403
www.balboapress.com
844-682-1282

Print information available on the last page.

ISBN: 979-8-7652-4185-1 (sc)
ISBN: 979-8-7652-4187-5 (hc)
ISBN: 979-8-7652-4186-8 (e)

Library of Congress Control Number: 2023908425

Balboa Press rev. date: 05/09/2023

CONTENTS

Princess
Poems

DEDICATIONS

To the dreamers
Whether they be wondrous and full of whimsy
Or wretched nightmares

A SPECIAL THANKS

To the inspiration of 'The Princess Poems'
The woman of whimsical ways
The lady of living dreams
The Princess of playful passion
FANCHETTE
Always be yourself

Phanathema: /fan'naTHema: the curse of being in
a dreamlike state, in particular nightmares.

PHANATHEMA

My fantasy and reality
Have merged into one.
I no longer taste love,
Nor the warmth of the Sun.
I sleep during the day,
And dream through the night.
I break through the glass,
And demolish the light.
The Moon is my savior,
The twilight my lord.
My prayers are unanswered
I have struck no accord.
A merger of powers,
A balance of life
The rain eats my pain,
The stars swallow my strife.
An occurrence, a dilemma,
Toward th end of my quest
No thoughts in my brain,
No heart in my chest.
So to my everlasting plight,
My final plea.
To hold the night,
Until the day is free.
The breathe in the air,

And recite to the Sun.
To search for excitement,
Then discharge my fun.
To hold all the clouds,
In the dot of my eye.
To replace all my hate,
With a baby blue sky.
Until the warmth of the day,
Returns to my veins.
I'll hold onto the black…

The Start of the End

Allow me to venture,
Inside of your brain,
Like a vagabond of thoughts
While you drift toward insane
I'm here to relieve you,
Except all your fears.
I'll alter your fantasies
You'll choke on the tears.
You wont feel any pain,
Close your eyes and lie down.
My existence is simple,
In this one story town.
Mercy in the hood,
My evils bring pain.
Heaven is sunshine,
And in Hell it is rain.
The end is near now,
It is time to face death,
As I whisper soft nothings,
Please take one last breath.
Let my cloak cover you,
And you rest in the pine.
The earth gets your body,
But your soul is mine.

THE EVE OF DEATH

The whispering wind wraps 'round his waist
His history haunts the human race.
The decisive demon of darkness and death,
Long livid livery and lowering breath.
He is:
The Ambassador of Annihilation
Premier of Passing
Dictator of Deceasing
Harvester of Harassing,
Phantom of Fatality,
Liquidator of Life,
Executioner of Essence,
Salesman of Strife,
The sickle holding slayer to which I bestow,
My mind, my heart, my body and soul.

DELI-KILL-TESSEN

Come in and sit down,
Please sample our treats,
No butcher in town,
Can compare with our meats.
They're juicy and fine,
They're supple and rare,
And, as I watch you dine,
You are unaware.
The meat that you test,
Has a secret of sorts,
And, while you digest
Consider the source.
You think that its steak,
You're sure that its cow,
But you've made a mistake,
And I'll tell you how...
My brother and I,
We were buried in debt,
With meat prices high,
And consumers upset.
So we drew up a plan,
A way to get by,
To pick out a man,
That we thought should die.

A vagabond, a vagrant,
A bum, to you and me,
Filthy and foul fragrant,
But, a price to be seen.
It started at first,
With a hobo or two.
Then we gained a thirst,
That just grew and grew.
So we handled the screams,
We dealt with the hollars,
To meet up with dreams,
And collect the dollars.
Soon, I took a liking,
To picking and choosing,
While he took a liking,
To killing, abusing.
Until late one night,
In the back slaughter room,
My brother in sight,
Brought on the gloom.
I didn't see it coming,
When he spoke his mind,
He was constantly humming,
Added lyrics and rewind.
'the men are roughest,
They fight to the death,
They all act the toughest,

'til their final breath.
The women, they're easy,
You just spike a drink,
Drop a pill, they feel queasy,
Then drain 'em in the sink.
But the kids you might feel,
Are the hardest to steal,
But they're easy to peel,
And we sell them as veal'
My terror was overwhelmed,
As he sung his song,
'Who is at the helm?
Why do I feel wrong?'
What scares me the most,
Is the butcher, my kin,
Though I am the host,
He wears the skin.
Then there is the trim,
On the side of this steak,
I couldn't control him,
Or the money we'd make.
So politely I said,
"You're in the deep end."
He went out of his head,
So, I had to pretend.
'Til a day in the fall,
When it all went wrong,

I had to make the call,
While he was singing his song.
We argued a bit,
With a push and a shove,
Enough of all this,
Raised the cleaver above…

A Riddle

I am in the hearts of children,
Excuse for lying tongues.
I understand your will and wish,
Your ladder without rungs.
I spin your brain,
confuse the eyes,
And make you slip away.
I twist the week,
I pull the month,
And make your day, today.
I chase your fears,
or make the up
But tripped a time or two.
But never fear,
I am right here,
And looking after you.
I have no touch,
no taste or smell,
And never can you see me.
But listen up,
Close your eyes,
And I'm certain you can hear me.
Can you hear me?
Did you listen?
Did you even try?

Do you know the answer?
Are you asking yourself why?
Or maybe you cant figure it.
If so, I apologize
If this riddle eludes you,
Then you are much too wise.
I need a favor from all of you.
Who think you know my name.
I've kept all of your secrets,
Could you keep mine all the same.

DRIFTING

I'm drifting away
But aren't we all.
We climb to the top,
And prepare to fall.
We sip our wine,
Its hard to swallow.
Revel in pain,
In hope, we wallow.
We never feel right,
If everything is good.
We abandon our souls,
To a man in a hood.
We present ourselves,
With passion and fear,
What we are afraid of,
Will never be clear.
We submerge one another,
With the dark waters,
Effecting our sons,
Hurting our daughters.
The time has come,
To rise up as one.
Stand proud on your feet,
Until you are done.
Don't wait on hope,

It will never arrive.
Be sure in your heart,
That you are alive.
Breathe in the air,
Be sure to smile,
And the man in the hood,
Won't come for a while.

TEN DAYS

Day one, at the club,
Just having some fun.
When this handsome man bought me a drink.
He made me feel easy,
Then I was queasy,
My brain just couldn't think.
I awoke on day two,
In some place new,
Shackled by chain to the wall.
This wasn't a dream,
I started to scream,
Didn't think I'd survive this at all.
Day three, I woke up,
To bread and a cup,
Water filled up to the brim.
Chilled to the bone,
Dark and alone,
And still there was no sight of him.
Then on day four,
Figure in the door,
A sinister smile on his face.
He never retreated,
As I cried and pleaded,
What he did next was disgrace.

Bruised but alive,

I think its day five,

He came in the room once again.

More beating and bruising,

Raping and abusing,

I hope that soon it will end.

Day six on my knees,

Begging God please,

I can no longer handle the pain.

Oh Lord, save me now,

Some way, Somehow,

When I found a weak link in the chain.

Day seven arrives,

With tears in my eyes,

I pulled and tugged on the chain.

And then on day eight,

It did separate,

As I waited for him with disdain.

No sleep on day nine,

As I paced the line,

'Til footsteps came up to the door.

With a swing and a crack,

A clink and a clack,

His body was left on the floor.

Nine days of terror,

And what's even unfairer,

Is a lifetime that's left fearing men.
They say I'll recover,
But to take on a lover…
I guess I'll approach that on day ten.

The Scientist

Lounge and loll, I must insist,
To tell the account of the scientist.
T'was in his study, behind the tome,
I had found the secrets of his home.
Flicker lit stairwell spiraling down,
You should have seen the sights I'd found.
'Hind the heavy webbed wooden slab,
I'd entered the doctor's secret lab.
Dust coated counters with beakers and books,
Jacob's ladders, test tubes, and hooks.
Chemicals and elixirs, dressed in line,
Drowning in scents of formaldehyde.
In the corner are cages rusted,
Filled with parts his anger lusted.
Bizarre implements all splashed with red,
Echoes and screams from those whom are dead.
Corroded creaking caught my ear,
I thought it best to disappear,
I ran, I hid and hunkered down,
As the doctor entered and panned around.
Silently, he paced the lab,
Staring down an empty slab.
He opened up a back room door,
Threw his patient to the floor.
She sobbed and moaned through muffled tones,

With bruises, scrapes and broken bones.
He circled 'round her as she lay,
Like predator that find their prey.
Frightened flesh on frozen floor,
Her strength was weak, her throat was sore.
Skin ripped against cold concrete,
With tired legs and lifeless feet.
Her hands were bound behind her back,
As he threw her on the porcelain stack.
He pushed her face, and strapped her down,
Then he donned a mask and gown.
He studied out his first incision,
As he cleaned his tools with such precision.
Rolling fluorescents on steel tray,
Instruments were on display.
Retractors, scalpels, needles and pins,
Forceps, skin hooks and a syringe.
The brain knife, the Liston, the Caitlin and saws,
Tappers, bone tamps, sutures and gauze.
With eyes aglow and brow oblique,
He demonstrated crazed technique.
Unveiled eyes exposed to light,
Bloodshot from tears, frozen by fright.
Awakened to fear, she began to seethe,
Heart rate shook, harder to breathe.
Rapid eye 'round the room,
Suddenly silenced, impending doom.
I stood in quiet, too scared to help,

As I turned away from her first yelp.
Flailing tools into the night,
Carving flesh, moonstruck delight.
The shine of silver slicing skin,
Behind the mask, a ghoulish grin.
Injecting liquids into her vein,
Cracking skull, exposing brain.
Wildly wielding her hair and head,
She'd probably is best off dead.
Gentle gray matter gashing,
Psycho cerebral slashing.
Then and there, a quarter's quiet,
The laboratory was completely silent.
And as for you, with stare agape,
A question comes, to my escape,
But lounge and loll I must persist,
Because I am the scientist.

ASHES

Butane, propane, kerosene
Ethanol, alcohol, gasoline
Carefully my scheme would hatch,
As soon as I would strike the match.
The sweet aroma filled the night,
As well as filling me with delight.
I can not help it, I love the burn,
I watched the flames as they would churn.
O' the flames, that unstoppable force,
I would watch them take their course.
I'd stare with glee, as it devoured,
Craved the strength that they empowered.
Its appetite is rarely picky,
Predicting its path, is rather tricky.
An arsonist is clearly crazed,
I was simply caught and dazed.
I love the fire, it burns within,
I wanted it to coat my skin,
Butane, propane, kerosene,
Ethanol, alcohol, gasoline.
I bought as many of them all,
And covered my room from wall to wall.
Forty-four tenants and burned 'em all,
I caroled as I soaked the hall,
I coated myself from head to toe,

Soon the smell would start to grow.
All I needed was a spark,
To start the trip I would embark.
I found my lighter, that good ole friend,
And lit it up to cause an end.
Orange and red tore up the place,
Torched my body and my face.
It ate through walls and raced through floors,
It melted windows and burned up doors,
I just stood there and watched it eat,
Lit up in fury, from head to feet.
Butane, propane, kerosene,
Ethanol, alcohol, gasoline.
My friends and I had done our work,
And you may think I went bizerk.
But trust me 'cause I kept my cool,
Until I heard the sound of fools.
Sirens screeching through the air,
Firefighters saved without a care,
They covered me with sheets of gray,
And told me that they'd save the day.
But when I said I want to burn,
To leave me be and don't return,
They ignored my scream and shout,
Ruined the day, they pulled me out,
I have these marks across my skin,
Ended the path I chose to begin.
I was so close to my destiny

Until they had to rescue me.
Butane, propane, kerosene,
Ethanol, alcohol, gasoline.
I'll never those fools for this,
I always knew it was hit or miss,
I went to court, they brought me here,
Maybe, my point was not made clear.
I wanted to burn, to be engulfed,
I had a plan and set it off.
An arsonist, I plead, I'm not,
I didn't even want a lot.
A simple request, that's not too rash,
To let me burn and fade to ash.
You all can have it that way too,
If you don't know how, than here's a clue.
Butane, propane, kerosene,
Ethanol, alcohol, gasoline.

PHANATHEMA II

Enter the snarling beasts,
Lightning in their eyes,
Thunder in their throats.
Heavy breath lingers in the corner.
Shadowed.
Fear creeps…
A fangled crawl across the floor.
Higher ground doesn't exist here.
It has been blackened by eclipsing plumage.
What are these evils of flight?
Where is my beacon of light?
Bleak despair, impending doom,
All stay with me inside this room.
Try as I might, out of bravery or fright,
My screams go unanswered still,
In this hullabaloo…
All hands are pocketed.

PRINCESS
POEMS

For Fanchette

The words float from my heart,
Up to my mind.
They are arranged
Sent down to my fingertips.
My hands wait impatiently to express them.
Then I wait..
To see if the feeling carries to You…

INTRODUCTION

There was nothing,
A wandering… unguided, mind you.
There was nothing,
A wondering… dreamlike and true.
For a time it seemed rancid,
Looking back, abysmal.
People came and went, passerbys,
Needing approval for my dismissal,
I trekked, solo, and finally perched,
Bleak and tried… oh so weak.
Curious of cowardice,
Refusals of smile and speech.
The long pressed arms stretching my lengths.
Inked with fallen memories.
Dust bowl of the northeast.
Acres waging wars against my body,
Over bearing, under whelmed,
Over taxed soul, underpaid heart,
Dirt settled and seed went in.
And as the blooms closed their heads,
Bowing out gracefully.
Dying out patiently.
The sky split, the light touched down,
Amongst the nearing decay.

The sights I'd found with short delay.
She wandered in, cast here,
Blue eyes aglow, lips sheer,
Stained by the kisses of angels.
Her presence lifted me,
From the depths of caverns forgotten,
She reached into the black,
Unknowing of her touch,
Unknowing of my loss,
A deep touch.
A touch into your soul, into mine,
Blindly releasing this glorious beam,
A glare of prismatic lights,
An aurora borealis in my chest.
She unleashed the wild animal that paced,
Inside hard caged links.
And in all of this… Her.
A smile to kiss the stars,
Eyes to light the way,
Out of clouded contempt.
A touch that felt like gentle wings,
Brushed across my skin.
A brighter life ahead.
And I will,
I will try to show her what she has done,
For me… to me.
I will show her brighter days

In her darker ones.
For the embers of a low glowing fire,
Smoldering at the end of my existence,
My voice will whisper soft at the dawn
I love you

TRAVELS

I have trekked the world,
Sights I have seen.
Far away and close.
Places I've been.
The breath of mountains,
The bath of seas,
But none can compare,
To the beauty of thee.
For I have traveled,
Searched night and day,
Nothing, near as wondrous,
Has come 'long my way.
Your lips so sweet,
When pressed to mine.
Your hair has it flows,
Like vivid black vine.
Your hands so small,
Rest soft on my skin.
Eyes drenched in blues,
I can see deep within.
Your skin, supple,
My lips come to crave.
To touch you all over,
Why must I behave.
To all of these sights,

That rest in my eye,
I have to admit,
I am ready to die,
To sweep through heaven,
Just to prove,
That even in the after.
Nothing is as gorgeous as you.

KALEIDOSCOPE

My eye is to your kaleidoscope,
The ever-changing shades,
A plethora of pigments,
From bright into haze.
A wonder aloft a river bed,
Eyes swallowed in blue,
A glimpse of her,
Spectral spectrum,
Astounded brilliance,
Sunrise over muted hum,
Her aura floats in and out,
Amongst the atmosphere,
Redefining nature's dyes,
And crossing through the clear.
Dipped in so much splendor,
I am a boy in a trance,
Twisting my kaleidoscope,
To watch those colors dance.

LULL

My arms wrapped around you,
The warmth between our bodies,
Between our heart beating.
The calm and comfort,
The beauty and sweet,
The words lingering in the air,
Waiting to be snatched up,
To be whispered in your ear.
I love you so much,
So gentle to touch,
Soft and tender embraces,
Looking into each other's faces,
Eyes connecting, deep stares,
Pushing away fears and cares.
Fingertips dancing and exploring,
Outside lost and ignoring,
Contained inside a cocoon of love,
Envied by the skies above.

PRINCESS' EYES

The deep dawn skies,
Possessed in her eyes,
The variations of blue,
Stretched out and through,
My fear of heights aside,
To take flight in a stride,
Destined for the depth,
Bounty and breath,
A moment to think,
Has been left there to drink,
Last droplet of water.
To die is no bother.
The gleam and glow,
Glint and glimmer resides,
This is the beauty,
In the princess' eyes.

SNUGGLES

Her strands of livid black,
Cast across her dove skin,
She giggles in-between kisses,
My arms dressing in,
Covering her bare breasts,
And the nape of her neck,
Becomes home for my chin.
Whilst my body is in check,
Forming the walls around her,
To protect her garden.
The blossomed and beauty,
Soft that will not harden.
Hands expressing interest,
Breaths becoming synced,
Natural and naked,
Moments where cheeks pinked,
Lost and found,
Nervous and sure,
Bodies so close,
The colors blur,
And deep beneath the surface,
The hearts beating,
From every embrace,
In our every meeting,

A love that endures,
A love so true,
Your love for me,
My love for you.

4 A.M.

It was a cold morning,
Four degrees,
I love the way that she warms me,
Such a tender heart,
It beats so deep,
I stopped and stared to watch her sleep.
The morning broke,
It shattered night,
Wrapped in blanket's plush delight.
The gorgeous princess,
Laid out in bed.
Dancing with dreams inside her head.
A midnight passed,
Bedtime was bliss,
It all began with an evening kiss.
But its 4 a.m.
My day's begun,
I'll let her sleep 'til the rising sun.

Drifting Thoughts of Her

Wrapped up in the thought of being
wrapped up with you...
Walking in the sun and morning dew,
Crisply roughed and toughed, my face.
Reminiscing and replaying her sweet taste.
Tempted but not whole,
Treated and not tricked,
Softly kissing her,
Lips stained and slicked.
Hair flowing black abound,
Rolling and rumbling 'round.
Testing the corners of my bed,
Thoughts of her in my head.
The beauty and grace of an angel,
As she dances in my mind,
Flowing livid hair fills the sky,
Laughs that get lost in time,
Her cheeks like that of cherubs,
Her lips taste like drops of love,
Her eyes are dazzling the sky,
Made from the wills above.
O' so grateful, is this man,
To touch te goddess of the moon,
To hold near and dear to him,
He hopes to embrace her soon.

Its time like this, I wish you were here,
Making more memories, expressing care,
The breaths and sighs while bodies were close,
Peering in through our eyes examining souls.
The night time drew in, heavy eyes laid to be,
And as you close yours, please dream of me…

LOVE LISTENING

Her intrigue is one which can not be defined,
Her sexual prowess is wild yet refined.
She prances deep with courtesy in my mind.
The chains of my heart unknowingly unwind.
Her whisper falls upon my ear,
With the precious words my soul endears.
Her voie is focal, background can not hear,
My defeats and decimations disappear.
For a moment with her is a diamond in time,
To linger the air in a song of chime,
Her eyes like the sky sapphire sublime,
And exhaled breath to make her mine.

The Beach

The best way to explain her,
Is the beach at night,
So shadowed at first,
Eyes adjust to moonlight.
Its on this point,
The moon to begin,
The glow and the white,
The same on her skin,
Serene flowing black,
The stars try to share,
Reminds me of lengths,
The stretch of her hair.
The scent of her strands,
Reside on my pillow,
Like glorious lines,
Weeping from the willow.
Her hands are soft,
Fingertips surely tell,
The story of waves,
That polished her shell.
They resemble the smooth,
And bury themselves,
When her hands tease mine,
I hear wedding bells,
The bell end droplets,

That shed from the sea.
The sea and those bells,
That she'll marry me.
The depths of her voice,
Conversing so deep,
Combined with the versing,
Her version of peep,
Remarkable woman,
Her flow and her ebb,
Her tides, her chicanes,
Her watery web.
Her lines ne'er crossing,
Her complex of course,
Creative, controlling,
Her complex of coarse.
The way that I feel,
To walk in this scene.
The changes of memory,
Death to serene.
The way that she twists,
Both body and wave,
Turns thoughts in my head,
Turvey my crave.

IF I COULD

If the moon were to be in full,
And the glow were to hit the tide,
In just the right way.
I would take a diamond,
Soak it in the wet,
Prismatically divide,
Split the colors down the seam,
And harness the brightest beam,
And if I were to keep that hue,
It wouldn't compare to you eyes of blue.

MORE SNUGGLES

The snuggles are the best,
These arms that guard her chest.
These hands that hold her breasts,
Protecting her precious heart.
Legs are entangled,
Hair can't be wrangled,
Bodies locked and angled,
Romance from the start.
Heavy weighted lids close eyes,
My leg wedged between her thighs,
This is where our love lies,
Our moments spent in part.
Part of some alluring dream,
Part of some cosmic scheme,
Love is bursting at the seam,
Destined from the start.

WHIMSICAL PLACES

From untold stories in hallowed woods,
To priceless boutiques and lavish goods,
From the swamps we've seen and prehistoric fish,
To hidden marsh and the Catskills squish,
From marble tiles and elevators of glass,
To the industry makers and a trip to class,
The hidden gazebo surrounded by boulders,
Skimming rocks before the weather turned colder,
The arboretum of spectrum and floral design,
To watching the twilight on horizon line.
The beaches, the mountains, the shacks and mansion.
The love that blossomed and began expansion.
From the kisses and holding hands together,
Through off season warmth and inclimate weather,
Each day is with whimsy, spontaneous on through,
But none of the places are as beautiful as you.

DAYDREAM

He sat there, just sat, boredom free flowing,
The sound of incessant tongue clucking laid the soundtrack
Another useless gathering of feeble minds.
His thoughts drifted in and out,
He began to stare, that good hard stare,
The one where the clock races by in peripherals,
The clock slowed.
A focal point.
A window.
Light refracting against a pitch black outside.
His silhouette.
Surrounded in the shine of energy saving lightbulbs,
Raindrops dancing across the pane,
Words floating in the air,
Dancing across his pain,
Two separate streams slipping side by side
Until.
Finally and softly they collide.
And there slips he,
Oft into thoughts of her.
Her smile.
Her laugh.
Her words.
Dreaming of diving into her eyes,
Like twilight mesh where weather and water meet.

Swimming in her dreams.
The rise and fall of her thoughts and emotions,
Riding the chicane of her heart,
This is where he floated.
Adrift in bliss.

THE BUTTERFLIES

Butterflies emerge,
As our interlaced fingers fan.
The same winged creatures,
That flutter inside me.
Bright feelings aglow,
New things to understand,
Something deep in her eyes,
Surfaces so sharply.
Softest of sapphires,
A powder ringed by steel,
Her hand pressed to mine,
In this magic moment,
Realizing the reality,
Reeling in all of this…real.
Waking the love,
That was so long dormant

Imagining You

I imagine,
Given the sleek style of your body,
It would be amazing stripped down,
Worthy of every inch to be tasted.
The way you move fills the air,
The scent of soft passion and sexy,
The accents of your curves leaves such an imprint,
An allure on my mind that causes me to stammer,
Typos over the words I desperately try to write.
The taste of your skin must be like sipping ambrosia,
Swallowing makes the gods mere mortals,
I feel every angel glares at you,
Aphrodite is consumed by envy and jealousy,
For nothing will best your phanallurment.

Solitude

I can not get the images out of my head,
That sexual being lying in my bed.
Her kisses left stains of romance on my lips,
My firm hands left imprints on her hips.
The nectar that lathers my tongue from her neck,
Laying here alone, my minds a wreck.
Her hair relaxed draped 'round her face,
I've never dreamed of such a place.
The clouds of pillows that we shared,
Vulnerable parts of our bodies shared.
The soft eyes.
Her tight thighs.
All rolling around in my brain.
The soundtrack of rain.
All this torture cuts to the bone,
As I lay here solemn and all alone.

A Reminder

I miss you, and if I should fall asleep forever,
Some words to remind you:
The words I say are crystal clear,
So, let them nuzzle in your ear,
Allow these words to settle in,
And see the light that shines within.
Know that I am always here,
To protect your soul from pain and fear.
I hold your heart so close to mine,
From here until the end of time.
So, when you rest inside your bed,
These words will kiss your weary head.

Each day you lift hearts up
With your magnificent conversations that illuminate,
A fire that can not be extinguished.
Your intellect and verbal passion is something to behold.
You're complex and cute,
A mixture of macabre and whimsy,
A unique individual that should
shine brighter than any star
Your beauty is incomparable,
You are a radiant flurry of different colors of light,
Light that shines deep into souls,
Into mine when I gaze into those snowy sapphires

Your smile.

It is elusive, sly, sweet, and full.

So many different ones.

Be yourself and smile,

Know who you are and be proud.

Do what makes you happy.